THE E-FUZZY ™

Words and pictures
© Marc Michaels 2017.

For my son Aryeh.

A sequel to the excellent
'Original Warm Fuzzy Tale'
by Claude M. Steiner.
Published with his kind permission.

A tale for everyone.

KULMUS
PUBLISHING

Kulmus Publishing
ISBN 978-0-9810947-5-5
Set in Bembo

there once was a lovely little village. It was very far away, but so very close to home, too.

It was a special place, where absolutely everyone who was born there, was given a soft blue bag to carry around. And, in the bag there was an inexhaustible supply of little round fluffy orangey-brown creatures.

These cute little bundles of love were known as **WARM FUZZIES**.

Whenever your family or your friends wanted to, they would reach into the bag and pull out a lovely **WARM FUZZY**. They would hand it to you gently and the little balls of fur would snuggle up into your neck, making you feel all warm and fuzzy and happppppy (with lots of 'p's) all over.

Well, once upon a time, there was a terrible battle between the children of the village and a nasty wicked witch. She had convinced all the adults that the **WARM FUZZY** supply might run out, so they started rationing them. The wicked witch was lying, because she wanted people to buy her useless potions instead - but unfortunately lots of people believed her. However, just in the nick of time, a lovely, kind lady, with flowers in her hair and who wore a long flowing skirt with sandals had come to the village. She reminded everyone there, that you can give a **WARM FUZZY** to anyone else at any time they want to and that they will never, *ever* run out.*

The really serious thing was that if no-one ever gave you any **WARM FUZZIES**, then there was a terrible danger that you could shrivel up and in some extreme cases, even die. You see, people needed **WARM FUZZIES** as much as they needed to eat and drink, or to breathe the air.

WARM FUZZIES were that important. Fortunately, it was really easy to give **WARM FUZZIES**. You could be a friend to a lonely elderly person. You could raise money for charity. You could just decide to do a random act of kindness for someone you knew, or even someone you just met. Or, you could simply spend time playing with your family and friends.

* If you would like to read the Original Warm Fuzzy Tale you can visit http://www.claudesteiner.com/fuzzy.htm

The adventure with the witch and the kind lady was a long time ago, but since then, some people became very good at giving out **WARM FUZZIES**, whilst other people kept them under lock and key, rarely sharing them with anybody else.

But now, because of the thirty year rule of

Ye Olde Warme Fuzzy Act,

I can share with you a never before told story.

Many years after the events of the original tale, the lovely little village had another visitor.

Not the evil witch. Not even an evil wizard or goblin, or ghost or ... well none of those types of thing, actually.

No.

The new visitor was a *businessman* and he was much worse than any of those scary made up pretend things - because he was real.

He was a bland looking grey haired, grey moustached man in a grey suit, wearing a bowler hat and carrying an umbrella. He was so very boring.

He never smiled or laughed and he had never, *ever* seen a **WARM FUZZY** before.

He certainly hadn't ever *given* a **WARM FUZZY** to anyone.

In fact, he wouldn't know a **WARM FUZZY** if it bit him on the leg. Which of course it wouldn't, as **WARM FUZZIES** just don't do that sort of thing.

Percival P. Popplethwaite III (for that was his name) was not an evil man, but he wasn't particularly nice either. All that mattered to him was his business and making money. He'd learnt that from his father Percival Popplethwaite II, who had learnt the very same lesson from his father – the first Percival Popplethwaite. No one knew what the extra 'P' stood for in the third Percival's name, but it was probably ... 'Profit'.

Percival was aware that some people managed to balance the time they spent at work with pleasant quality time shared with their families and friends. He had seen it with his own eyes, so it must be true. But, he didn't really feel it was for him. Any time that he wasn't making money was time wasted, as far as he was concerned. Indeed, at that very moment, he was wasting a great deal of time and money, for his *super-stretch* limousine had broken down. He was stranded in some little village, in the middle of nowhere. His driver was trying to fix the car, with little success and Percival was getting very impatient. He decided to go for a walk or else he was likely to shout at the driver – a lot – and that would probably delay him even more.

Percival reluctantly left his car and went for a stroll around the little village. He hoped it wouldn't be long before he could begin work once again. It literally hurt him to think of all the money that he might be losing.

It was the same thing for Percival every single day. He never switched off from the moment he awoke to the moment his head hit his pillow.

If he could have worked out a way to avoid having to sleep, he would have. That way, he could be sure of making the most money he possibly could.

Grasping his 'brolly firmly in his hand, he proceeded to march up and down the village. He looked everywhere - but saw nothing - since he totally failed to notice just how pretty, quiet and peaceful everything was.

Instead, he thought to himself, how well organised, efficient and cost-effective the sewage and drainage systems were. He was also getting really quite excited about the prospect of the Targets and Penalty Clauses that the legal contract might contain.

It wasn't just that Percival didn't know how to enjoy himself and relax for the briefest of moments, it was that he really didn't want to. It just never occurred to him that that was a worthwhile way to spend his time.

And so, Percival missed out on life's simplest pleasures each and every single day.

Then, Percival spotted some children playing together in a nearby field. They laughed and jumped and ran around, holding hands. They seemed so very happy, that even Percival seemed curious as to why.

He noticed the little blue bags on belts that they all wore. He also wondered about the strange bright orangey-brown fluffy balls that clung onto the children's shoulders, snuggling into their necks as they played in the sun.

They really were very happy and he just couldn't understand why that was. They didn't appear to be making any money running around like that, either for themselves or - more importantly - for him. It just didn't seem natural to him. Very odd behaviour indeed, he thought.

Percival moved closer to the children and, without a moment's hesitation, reached out and just grabbed a **WARM FUZZY** from the shoulder of one of the children.

The **WARM FUZZY** gave a little shriek of fear as it was pulled away. Percival P. Popplethwaite III didn't seem to care one little bit.

"What is this?" he asked slowly and precisely in a monosyllabic voice that showed no emotion.

The children, who were a little scared, started falling over each other in an effort to back away from the strange, grey man. Charlie, however, was brave and stepped forward to confront the grey stranger.

Percival looked down at Charlie.

Charlie looked up at Percival.

"It's a **WARM FUZZY**"
he answered.
"A Warm what?"
"Fuzzy sir," replied Charlie.
"Well, what is it for?
What's its purpose?"
Percival believed
everything had to
have a purpose,
or it was wasteful
and inefficient and
should be
shut down
immediately.
"It makes you feel
all warm and fuzzy
all over,"
explained Charlie.

Percival was taken aback and, for the very first time in several months, his face betrayed an actual emotion. A glint of greed crept into his eyes. Hmm, he thought, a product that makes people happy ... immediately. How amazing.

"And how much does it cost?"

"Cost?" Charlie spluttered.

Charlie had no idea what the tall, grey man was talking about. Instead, Charlie stood there with his mouth hanging open. The rest of the children looked at the grey man as if he were mad - which he may well have been.

"They don't cost sir. They're free of course. You just *give* them to your friends when you want to," replied Charlie, quite amazed at the question.

"Free. Hmm. Well, in that case, you won't mind me having this one, will you?"

Percival marched off towards a local hotel, carrying the **WARM FUZZY**. The children were appalled. For someone to just *take* a **WARM FUZZY** was simply unheard of.

Later that night, Percival locked the poor **WARM FUZZY** in a cage that he put at the foot of his bed. For once, he slept soundly, snoring heavily, dreaming of the oodles and oodles of money, that he was going to make.

As soon as his *super-stretch* limousine was repaired, he hurried back to his factory in the **Big City**.

Once there, he summoned scientists from his company's well-equipped and expensive laboratories.

Later that day, they began to organise a series of very, very, VERY unpleasant tests with laser beams and all sorts of other odd equipment to be carried out on the poor **WARM FUZZY**, who was absolutely terrified.

It was just horrible ... absolutely horrible.

Percival didn't care – not one little bit. After all, there was profit to be made.

Percival P. Popplethwaite III pushed his staff very hard indeed, making them work around the clock. He wasn't at all nice and shouted at them down the 'phone quite a lot. But he still didn't care.

Eventually, the scientists and economists produced a one thousand page report on the 'Economic Viability Of Mass Fuzzy Production'. It was packed with lots of graphs and tables and many appendices, detailing the process by which **WARM FUZZIES** could be man-made in great quantities and sold at shockingly high prices.

And so the new product started churning off the assembly lines at an alarming rate.

Passing along conveyor belts to be packed into special plastic containers and shipped out across the world to the high street shops and out of town hyper-markets.

But these weren't real **WARM FUZZIES** at all.

Oh yes, they smiled and looked happy enough - but they were only ... **E-FUZZIES**™.

After all, you didn't need anyone to *give* you it. If you had enough money (and you did need to save up an awful lot), you could go to the store, choose and buy your very own E-FUZZY™.

Then you would go home, plug it in and play with it, sitting alone in your room, or even alone with your friends, staring blankly at it, shooting at it, watching it, or listening to it, depending on what particular model of E-FUZZY™ you had decided to buy.

Children, in particular, started spending endless hours alone in their rooms, swiping screens and pressing buttons and looking – a little vacantly, it must be said – at their **E-FUZZIES™**.

They often completely forgot about their friends and sharing real **WARM FUZZIES**.

It was very, VERY sad indeed.

Having swamped the market with millions of **E-FUZZIES™**, Percival made sure that every so often they would just fall apart - a thing he called 'built in obsolescence'. Then he would advertise the latest upgrade with completely unnecessary extra special components in an effort to get you to go out and buy replacement **E-FUZZIES™**. He made portable ones so that they could be taken anywhere - just like the original **WARM FUZZIES**.

Indeed lots of people thought that their **E-FUZZIES™** were great. Sometimes they were - you could share stuff with people far away, you could find out things easily and you could have a bit of fun. Well, they weren't bad in themselves ... mostly, but people did spend rather a lot of time with them and forgot about some of the more important things in life. They sat around a lot and got a bit fatter. They couldn't concentrate as much. Some people got a bit depressed, finding it difficult to be without their **E-FUZZIES™**, constantly checking them. And, whilst they didn't shrivel up, perhaps their brains shrunk a bit.

Meanwhile in the lovely little village, Charlie's friends continued to give each other **WARM FUZZIES**. However, from what he could see, not as much as they used to. They also seemed to be spending too much time alone with their **E-FUZZIES™**. This worried Charlie, but something else was worrying him even more.

Something that had been worrying him ever since the fateful day that the grey man had taken the **WARM FUZZY** from his shoulder. Normally Charlie wouldn't worry about **WARM FUZZIES** that he'd given away, as he knew the person who had received the **WARM FUZZY** would love it dearly and take good care of it until it was time to pass it onto another friend.

For days afterwards, Charlie had convinced himself that perhaps the grey man would still treat the **WARM FUZZY** well. After all, they were so fluffy and smiley, that surely even the grim looking grey man would fall under its spell. It would have snuggled up to him and as its warm fuzziness got to work, the man would break into a huge smile himself and bitterly regret having taken it.

It was Charlie's way to think the best of everyone. It was this thought that allowed Charlie to feel a bit better about the whole incident. Yet, as days turned into weeks, he just couldn't get rid of the nagging doubt that all was not well with the little **WARM FUZZY**.

It was shortly after the **E-FUZZIES™** had first appeared in the local shops that Charlie finally made up his mind to do something. He wasn't sure what he was going to do, but somehow he knew he needed to rescue the **WARM FUZZY**.

Charlie tried to gather his friends together. Some of them didn't want to come, as they said they were busy with their **E-FUZZIES™**. This worried Charlie even more than he had been. Had some of his friends forgotten what was really important?

Charlie's parents had offered to buy him his own **E-FUZZY™** too. However, he didn't really want one. He preferred real **WARM FUZZIES**, playing outside with friends, running around, climbing trees and playing sports.

His aunt Lucy had eventually bought him a cheap starter model, as even the Olde Village Shoppe, that his mum and dad ran, had started selling them.

He had turned it on and it had smiled at him, but it just felt false and a bit unreal. After a few minutes Charlie put it in the top drawer in his bedroom.

Maybe he would play with it in a few weeks time. Maybe not.

The next day, two of Charlie's best friends, Jasmine and Aryeh, came round to his house for tea after school. They gathered in Charlie's bedroom and he told them about his concerns that the **WARM FUZZY** that the grey man had taken might not be being properly cared for. They found it hard to believe. They just couldn't imagine anyone being deliberately nasty to a **WARM FUZZY**. However, they soon agreed that they had to come up with a plan.

Charlie announced that he had already done some homework. He had seen an article about the grey man in a magazine on his dad's desk. It said that he ran a company called Popple and that it was the same man who had invented the **E-FUZZY**™. It also mentioned his name was Percival P. Popplethwaite III and that he had been inspired when he had visited a quaint little village in the middle of nowhere. It didn't mention that he had stolen a **WARM FUZZY**, but then Charlie suspected that wouldn't have made such a good story for Popple to sell its products. It said Popple's main headquarters was in the **Big City**, so that that's where Charlie thought the **WARM FUZZY** was most likely to be.

"But how is that going to help us?" asked Jasmine. "We can't go into a huge factory in the **Big City**. We're just children."

"Yes," added Aryeh, "and they will have badges and big security guards and fences and ferocious guard dogs and maybe fire breathing dragons and ..."

SPECIAL FEATURE

PERCIVAL P. POPPLETHWAITE III

INVENTOR OF THE E-FUZZY™

WHAT'S THE SECRET BEHIND HIS SUCCESS?

"We're not breaking in," interrupted Charlie, "but we *are* going to that factory."

"How?" chorused his two friends.

"Well," continued Charlie, "at the end of the article, it said that Popple was running special tours for school children. It was part of a programme that they had created to convince young people to grow up and join the company." It seemed that Mr Popplethwaite thought that children were very creative and had the best ideas. But, again he didn't say in the article that he'd stolen those ideas.

"And," explained Charlie, "we can write a letter that says our school would like to send three pupils who really would like to be part of the 'Popple success story'. They are sure to let us in and when they're not watching, we'll leave the tour, split up and look for our **WARM FUZZY**."

"Sounds like a good plan," said Aryeh excitedly.

"Well, yes, but it's probably a big factory and there are only three of us and we don't know where to look. Also, we won't have much time before the tour guides miss us. So it may be a bit harder than I'm making it sound," warned Charlie.

"Still a good plan," exclaimed Aryeh, already bravely forgetting about the security dragons.

"It is a plan," agreed Charlie. "We'll see if it is a *good* one if we rescue the **WARM FUZZY**."

On the day of the tour, the three children removed their little blue bags, just in case the grey man recognised them. Charlie's parents took them to the Popple factory in the **Big City**.

The tour guide was a nice, well dressed older lady with long hair and a kindly smile. She welcomed them and the other children. The parents were told the tour would be just over an hour, but that there were many exciting places where they could grab a bite to eat in the **Big City**. They could then collect their children at the end of the tour, back in the entrance lobby.

Charlie did a quick count. There were just under fifty children, so perhaps they wouldn't notice if three went missing briefly. If they were missed, they could always say they got lost, since all the corridors looked the same. He didn't know if all the corridors did look the same, but, given how boring the grey man had been, he suspected that this might be the case. They would just have to have their wits about them and take the first chance they had to make their move when the time came.

In fact, they didn't even need to leave the group. One of the early stops on the visit was Percival's very own recently redecorated office.

There was a huge ornate wooden desk and, hanging behind it, three large portraits of three men. They all looked very similar to Percival. In fact one was Percival, but without his bowler hat on. The other two looked just like him, except they had more elaborate facial hair. The nice tour guide lady explained who the three Popplethwaites were and how important they were. On another wall, there was a big screen with numbers showing sales figures for **E-FUZZIES**™ and how much money this was making for Popple.

The numbers were spinning so fast that you could hardly make them out before they changed. Percival was getting very rich, very quickly.

But Charlie, Jasmine and Aryeh were not looking at the portraits or the screen or the spinning numbers. They weren't even looking *at* the desk, but *under* it. As, almost out of sight, in the shadows under the grand old mahogany desk, was a small bird cage. In the cage was a small fuzzy shape - though it looked kind of pale and not its normal healthy orangey-brown. It was the missing **WARM FUZZY**! What was odd, thought Charlie, was the door to the cage was open and yet the **WARM FUZZY** hadn't even tried to escape. In fact, it wasn't even moving. Perhaps it was just asleep? But why would Percival leave the cage open? It was almost like he had completely forgotten about the **WARM FUZZY**.

So, thought Charlie, we don't have to pick a lock - not that any of them knew how to pick a lock anyway - but how on earth were they going to get under the desk in full view of the nice tour guide lady and the other children.

What nobody knew was that, at that very moment, Percival P. Popplethwaite III had arrived at his horrible smoke-belching factory in his chauffeur driven *super-stretch* limousine.

Suddenly the door to the office burst open. In marched Percival P. Popplethwaite III. He looked extremely annoyed.

"I specifically said this part of the tour needed to be finished by 2.32 p.m. precisely," he announced angrily to the tour guide lady who immediately turned a nasty shade of pale green. "And," continued Percival tapping impatiently on his watch, "it is now precisely 2.33 p.m. and there are still children in my office. Remove the children at once and then remove yourself. Consider yourself fired."

The tour guide lady started shaking and hurriedly started shooing the children towards the door. She hoped that by getting the children out of the office as quickly as possible, that she would keep her job. She was wrong. Percival was still in the way of the door and he was surrounded by loads of children who were all trying to get out of small opening in a mad rush. Children ran into Percival's legs and started falling over themselves. He stood there red-faced.

Charlie spotted his opportunity. He signalled to his friends to stand together in front of the desk. He dived between their legs under the desk, scooped up the motionless **WARM FUZZY** from out of the cage, placed it gently into his pocket and quickly came up to stand beside his friends, trying to look all angelic and innocent.

Fortunately, in all the confusion, no-one noticed Charlie's athletic rescue moves. Instead, all the children continued filing out of the door whilst Percival got angrier and angrier. You wouldn't know it, but he was actually trying very hard to control his temper, as even he knew that shouting at children – his best customers – would be bad for business. However, you could see how he was getting even redder and redder in the face as he bottled up his rage.

The tour guide lady was counting the children out. "Forty six, forty seven ..."

She turned round to see the final three children standing by Mr Popplethwaite's desk.

"Come along now children. We don't want to keep Mr Popplethwaite waiting. He has very important work-related things to do."

Popplethwaite grunted impatiently, looking at his watch again pointedly. Charlie and his two friends inched away from the desk cautiously and then past the tour guide and Percival. As Charlie passed Popplethwaite their eyes met briefly.

"Do I know you?" asked Popplethwaite suddenly. "I don't recall knowing any actual children, but you seem very familiar."

That's it, thought Charlie ... the game's up.

"Errr," stammered Charlie, "errr."

"He looks a bit like a younger Brian Simpkins sir," volunteered the tour guide lady bravely.

"Who?" barked Popplethwaite.

"Brian Simpkins, sir. You know, the young man who just started working in the post-room. You met him very briefly on Monday. Very briefly. You must be confusing them."

"Oh, that idiot," tutted Percival. "That young whippersnapper didn't even address me as 'sir.' He will probably stay in the post-room until he retires, I expect."

Percival looked down dismissively at Charlie.

"On your way child," he announced, "I have money to make. I've just lost four and a half minutes. Heaven knows how it has affected the company's profits."

Charlie moved quickly past Popplethwaite, out of the office and into the endless grey corridors. The office door swung shut and Charlie finally breathed out. He had been holding his breath since the tour guide lady had interrupted and he hadn't even noticed. He quickly felt inside his pocket.

The **WARM FUZZY** was still there.

The tour guide lady bent down to him, winked and whispered, "I'm not going to admit to knowing what it was, but it looked really sick to me and I'm sure it is going to a better home. I don't like cages."

She had seen the whole thing and hadn't said a single word.

"Thank you," gasped Charlie.

She led them back to the entrance, where each child was given a goody bag full of Popple merchandise, including **E-FUZZY™** shaped sweets and a voucher for (oddly) 6.5% off their next **E-FUZZY™** purchase.

The parents arrived and collected their children. Finally outside the factory, Charlie and his two friends breathed another huge sigh of relief. The plan hadn't been that good, but they had been very lucky and it had worked.

They had rescued the **WARM FUZZY**.

But the **WARM FUZZY** didn't look like it had been rescued. In fact, it didn't look like it even knew it had been rescued. It was almost as grey and lifeless as Charlie remembered Mr Popplethwaite being on the day they had first met. It lay there completely still, cupped in the palm of Charlie's hand.

"Perhaps it'll get better if we each sing a song to it, or play a game and invite it to join in," ventured Jasmine. "After all, that's when **WARM FUZZIES** are at their happiest – when everyone is having a good time. Perhaps it will hear us and wake up."

So they each took turns singing a little song, but nothing happened. The **WARM FUZZY** just lay there motionless.

"What if we sing together."

So they tried that and still nothing happened.

"We could play catch?" suggested Aryeh. "I've got a tennis ball in my pocket."

"Why did you bring a tennis ball?" asked Charlie.

"I thought that if things got a bit hairy, I could throw it at the security dragon and when it hit it on the nose, it would run away."

Charlie smiled. Aryeh had a great imagination.

So they started playing catch, but their hearts weren't really in it. The **WARM FUZZY** looked like it had been drained of all its fuzziness and this just wasn't enough to revive it.

"I saw it move," cried Jasmine, "just a little bit." But it was wishful thinking – the **WARM FUZZY** still looked a deathly cold grey colour.

The children were racking their brains for a better solution. Perhaps, they would have more luck when they were back in the lovely little village and far away from the very noisy and somewhat smelly **Big City** factory. There would certainly be a lot more families to join in with games, which should help rouse the poor, unfortunate **WARM FUZZY**.

They were just about to leave when Charlie noticed the tour guide lady leaving the building. She looked very sad. Charlie thought she might be crying a little. She was moving slowly towards the car park, dabbing at her eyes with an old-fashioned lace handkerchief.

He rushed up to her, still holding the **WARM FUZZY** gently in his palm.

"Wait, tour guide lady. Wait. Please."
She paused, just as she was opening her car door.
"Wait!" said Charlie again, even more urgently.
She turned around and smiled at him.

"What can I do for you young man?" she asked.
"Well," said Charlie, "I just saw you coming out of the office and you looked very sad. I heard what Mr grey m... Mr Popplethwaite said to you. You didn't really lose your job, did you?"

The tour guide lady smiled again. She had a kindly smile that would light up a room.

"Yes, I'm afraid I did. Once Mr Popplethwaite says he'll do something, well, you can consider it done. There are no second chances with Percival P. Popplethwaite III!"

"But that's terrible," sighed Charlie, crestfallen. "We didn't mean for you to lose your job."
"Oh, it wasn't you. Don't fret about it. It wasn't a very nice job anyway. I'm not sure I was cut out to work in a **Big City** factory," she explained, "when I was much younger, I used to be something of a hippy - you know flower garlands in my hair, long patterned floral skirts, sandals and that sort of thing.

I used to go from village to village, singing, sharing stories, taking on evil witches ..." she said, thinking back fondly.

"Did you say wit..." Charlie tried to interrupt, his mouth dropping open in surprise. But the tour guide lady carried on speaking.

"... and occasionally working in little village shops to make ends meet. Maybe I'll go back to doing that."

Charlie didn't quite understand what a hippy was. However, he had seen old pictures of his grandpa Tim and grandma Margaret dancing in fields wearing those sorts of outfits. The pictures always made them feel happy, like they were remembering extra special times. Charlie liked seeing them happy.

"My mum and dad run the Olde Village Shoppe!" exclaimed Charlie. "You should come to live in our village. I'm sure they'll have a job for you."

"Well that's very kind said the tour guide lady. Maybe I'll have a chat with your parents and see what's possible. Anyway, it might be a bit early to start talking about new jobs when I don't even know your name?"

"Charlie," said Charlie.

"And I'm Janet," replied the tour guide lady who crouched down to Charlie's height and offered him her hand.

Charlie reached out to shake her hand, completely forgetting he was still holding the **WARM FUZZY**. He stopped and then he offered Janet the **WARM FUZZY**.

"Here," he said, "you need this."

Suddenly and without warning, there was this bright orange sparkly glow and the **WARM FUZZY** sprang back to life in Charlie's hand, leapt up onto Janet's shoulder, snuggling into her neck.

As the **WARM FUZZY** nuzzled his new friend, Charlie grinned. He understood. **WARM FUZZIES** needed to be *given*. They simply didn't work if they were stolen or bought.

So Charlie, his parents, Aryeh, Jasmine, his new friend Janet and the rescued **WARM FUZZY** all went back to the lovely little village. They told everyone about their adventure and the wonderful feeling that the gift of a real **WARM FUZZY** could bring.

Percival P. Popplethewaite III continued to watch his money grow and grow. After all, that's all that mattered to him. They never saw him again.

Most people continued to play with their **E-FUZZIES™** and whilst they had their uses, some of them spent far too much time with them. Some scientists (the ones who didn't work for Popple) said that this was doing them quite a lot of harm, but most people just ignored that.

Some people, however, were a bit more thoughtful and realised that seeing their friends and relatives, playing in the park, going to youth groups, going off to camp, playing sport, playing musical instruments, helping out at the old-age home and putting aside their **E-FUZZIES™** for a while would be a really good idea. Some people restricted the time they spent with their **E-FUZZY™** each day to a few hours only. Others tried to have a break away from their **E-FUZZY™** and turn them off for at least one day a week and concentrate on sharing real **WARM FUZZIES** as much as they could.

And most children, who started to enjoy fresh air, exercise, fun and proper real **WARM FUZZIES** then realised ...

... that their super slim, shiny, new feature-packed **E-FUZZIES™** just weren't as good as the real thing.

And, whilst they didn't get rid of them, they played with them an awful lot less ... you know, when it was a bit rainy outside.

The End

'... since most people's power
of giving remains at a low level
they tend to restrict their giving
and their love
to a narrow circle
of relatives and friends ...
[but] if I give to someone,
I feel close to them;
I have a share in their being.
it follows that if I were
to start bestowing good
upon everyone
I come into contact with,
I would soon feel that
they are **all** my relatives,
all my loved ones.
I now have a share
in them all ...'

R. Eliyahu Dessler
Strive for Truth, Volume 1, p.130

About this book

This book began life as a story that I wrote as a youth leader at a children's summer camp back in the 1980s. However, it wasn't until 2007, that I finally plucked up courage to write to Claude Steiner, to ask him if he would like to collaborate on a sequel. This is what he kindly wrote back:

> Dear Marc,
>
> I am working on two other tales. One on lying and the other on power abuse but I have not thought of writing a sequel to the WFT. You are free to publish the one you wrote (good concept I feel) providing that you give credit for its source.
>
> Good luck with your project and keep me informed.
>
> Fuzzies
> Claude Steiner

I did send him a couple of drafts, which I sincerely hope he enjoyed, but I never got to send him the final version, as unfortunately, he passed away on 10th January 2017. His final words were "love is the answer" and then "I am so lucky". A very special man indeed.

At the time I first drafted the story, I called it the Electronic Fuzzy and the one I had in mind was the TV. However, over time things have moved on and Digital, Virtual or E-Fuzzies come in all shapes and sizes. PCs, laptops, game consoles, tablets, smart-phones, virtual reality headsets, wearable 'tech' and portable digital devices of all kinds. You name it, it will be on a screen.

Now, as the book says, the E-Fuzzies aren't in themselves bad, but some of the behaviours that they create can be. What is needed is a more balanced approach - a golden mean, so to speak. A way where technology does enhance our lives without taking away the beauty of human companionship and the simple physical pleasure of friends playing in the park - not to mention the healthy exercise that promotes too - and just helping other people. Constant exposure to screens is certainly changing the way we all think and see the world, but not necessarily always for the better.

My thanks therefore go to Claude Steiner for his excellent Original Warm Fuzzy Tale, that inspired me to write this sequel and for his very kind permission to allow me to publish this. If you haven't read the original, go and find it now. My thanks to children's author Jordan Stratford for his comments on a draft that wasn't quite right, and I knew it, but needed someone else to tell me to get back to my original ideas. Thanks also to Julian Perkins for his expert proof-reading.

My thanks also, to my son Aryeh, who proof-read and who worked with me, some time ago now, to move the idea of the E-Fuzzy from my head and onto ... yes, a computer screen. See they aren't bad ... just misunderstood.

Marc Michaels, 2017

About the author/illustrator

Marc Michaels has spent most of his working life as a marketing communications professional. For over a quarter of a century of that he worked for the Central Office of Information (COI), helping run behavioural campaigns that aimed to save and improve people's lives and 'make a real difference'.

Marc is also a practicing scribe (*Sofer STa"M*). This involves writing, and restoration work on, sacred manuscripts written on parchment with a feather quill. His scribal website is at www.sofer.co.uk.

About the source of inspiration

Claude Michel Steiner was a French-born American psychotherapist, a founder and practitioner of Radical Psychiatry.

As a writer he focused on transactional analysis which aims to get everyone to 'adult' independence and a sense of their own and of other's inherent value.

He examined learnt early life scripts, alcoholism, emotional literacy, and interpersonal power plays. His Warm Fuzzy Tale looked at social interaction and gave the world the term 'warm fuzzies' to describe positive feelings. In it, he stressed the importance of freely giving to, and asking from others.

He was the 'giant' whose shoulders I have been fortunate enough to stand upon.

Photo kindly supplied by Dr. Noemi 'Mimi' Doohan, Claude Steiner's daughter.